WE BE WARM
TILL SPRINGTIME COMES

by Lillie D. Chaffin/illustrated by Lloyd Bloom

MACMILLAN PUBLISHING CO., INC., NEW YORK
COLLIER MACMILLAN PUBLISHERS, LONDON

Macmillan Publishing Co., Inc.
866 Third Avenue, New York, N.Y. 10022
Collier Macmillan Canada, Ltd.
Printed in the United States of America
10   9   8   7   6   5   4   3   2   1

Library of Congress Cataloging in Publication Data
Chaffin, Lillie D
We be warm till springtime comes.
Summary: Young Jimmy Jack Blackburn
searches for fuel to keep his mother and baby sister
warm through a severe Appalachian winter.
[1. Fuel—Fiction. 2. Winter—Fiction.
3. Appalachian region—Fiction] I. Bloom, Lloyd.
II. Title. PZ7.C3485We   [E]   80-12380   ISBN 0-02-717910-9

For Jackie, Nikki and Christa Chaffin—
may they always have springtime
—L.D.C.
For Cyndy, my wife
—L.B.

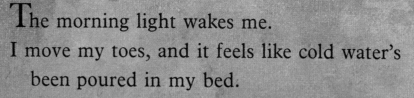

The morning light wakes me.
I move my toes, and it feels like cold water's
   been poured in my bed.
"Woo-eee, it's cold enough to freeze the whiskers
   off a monkey," I say.
"Think about summer," Mama says,
   "and if summer seems too far off,
   think about when springtime comes."

I think, but it doesn't help much.
The shivers are still on my shoulders.
The tingles are still in my fingers.
The numbness is still in my feet.

The world is one big iceberg.
It is one big windstorm and snowball.
And we're on top of it.

We are Mama and Baby Mary and myself,
   Jimmy Jack Blackburn.
Our fireplace is a giant dragon that gobbles up
   coal and wood.
It breathes out a little heat.
When we don't feed the fire, it dies.

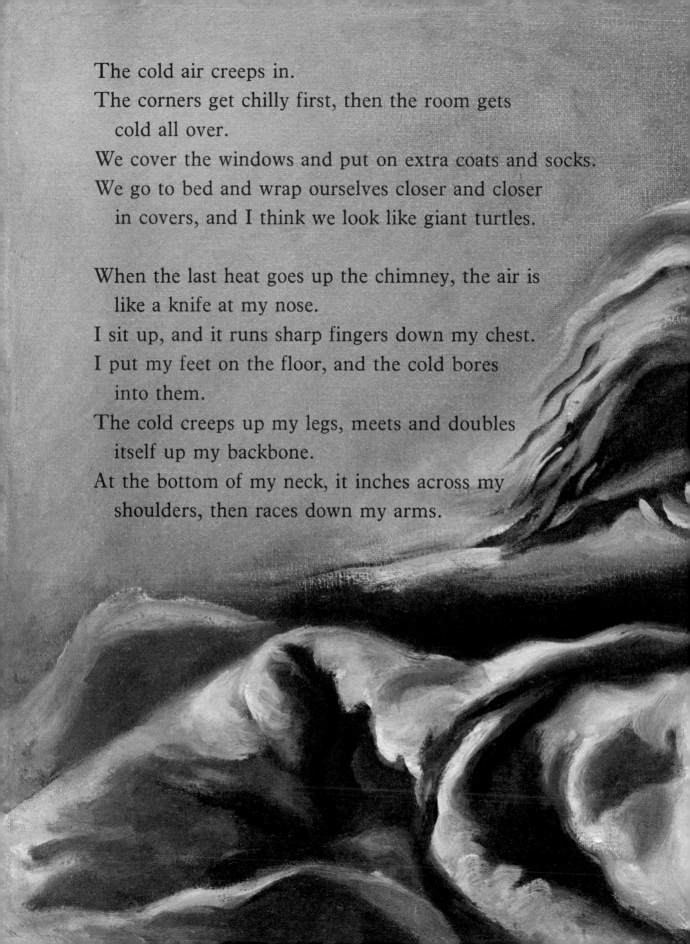

The cold air creeps in.
The corners get chilly first, then the room gets
 cold all over.
We cover the windows and put on extra coats and socks.
We go to bed and wrap ourselves closer and closer
 in covers, and I think we look like giant turtles.

When the last heat goes up the chimney, the air is
 like a knife at my nose.
I sit up, and it runs sharp fingers down my chest.
I put my feet on the floor, and the cold bores
 into them.
The cold creeps up my legs, meets and doubles
 itself up my backbone.
At the bottom of my neck, it inches across my
 shoulders, then races down my arms.

I could sit on a hot stove, if we had one.
I could drink a gallon of hot chocolate, hot soup,
  hot tea.
But we don't have enough coal or wood for heating
  anything, and the sun is hiding behind clouds,
  and the wind is whining and scratching at
  the cracks in the house.

"Oh, woo-eee, it's cold in here," I say.
Mama sticks her head above the covers in the bed
across the room and says, "Don't wake the baby.
Law, it is cold, and we've used up all the coal
and nearly all the wood. This may be the worst cold
spell we ever had. We be cold till springtime comes,
Jimmy Jack."

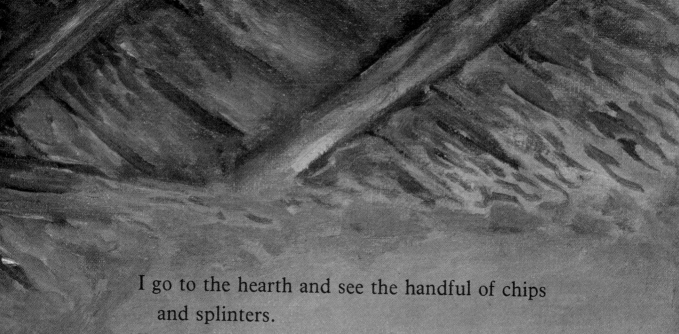

I go to the hearth and see the handful of chips
   and splinters.
"There's just one thing to do," I say.
"And what's that?" Mama asks.
"Get us some heat-makers."

"Sure would be nice," Mama says, "but where do we
   get heat-makers?"
"Might find some coal up on the hill," I say.
"Be hard for me to get up there with just these
   old rag shoes," Mama says.
"I got big heavy shoes that could go to the North
   Pole," I say.
"You're not big enough to dig coal," Mama says.
"I'm big enough to freeze to death," I tell her,
   "but I'm not going to."

I load the rusty old toy wagon with the stuff

I push and pull, push and slide, up about a foot,
    slide back about six inches, using that old pick
    like a cane.
Sometimes I stop and catch the heat that goes out
    of me against one hand and then the other one.

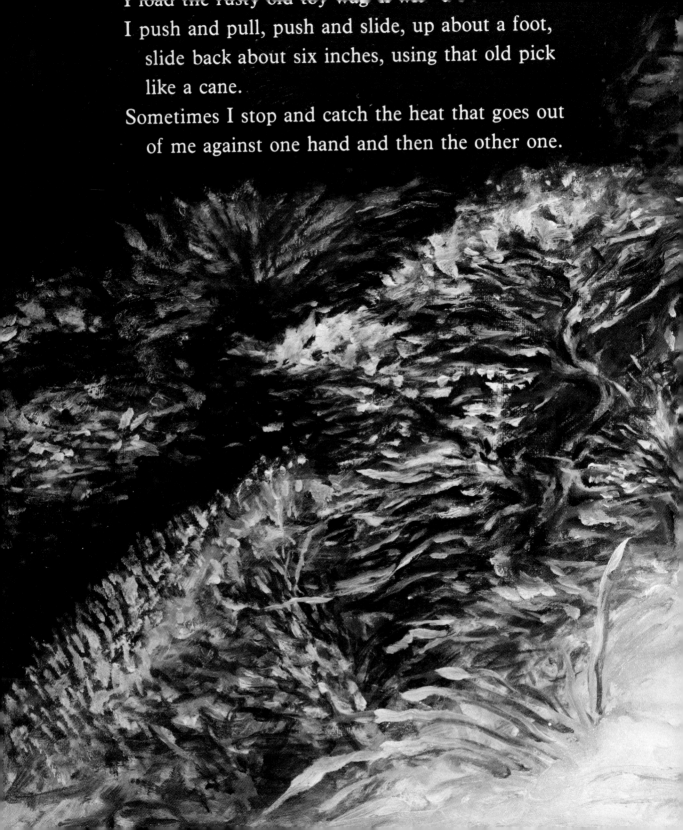

Then I'm at the hole in the hill we call
   a coal bank.
Long ago somebody dug coal from this hole.
I put a rock under the wagon wheels and peek back
   into the hole.

The floor is water, and the ceiling is rock.
It's darker in there than two midnights put together.
A big old tree is standing nearby.
It moves a little when the wind blows against it.
Some of the limbs are creaking dry.

I squat between the water and rock and feel like the
   storybook mouse in the lion's paw, like a rabbit
   running into a deadfall trap.
If the top falls, it'll squash me out like a stepped-on bug.
"Don't you dare fall on me," I say. Then I add, "please."

I lift the pick and swing it into a bunch of coal.
A piece breaks away and falls and smashes.
Wham, wham, I bang into the coal, and I get almost
   hot enough to pull off my coat.

After a while I pick up the lumps and drop them
    into the wagon.
I shovel up the smaller pieces.
The wagon tries to run away as I scoot downhill.

"Look, here's a whole big coal pile," I say,
    kind of joking.
It's not really that big, but it looks big when
    Mama smiles.
She puts a wad of paper and some splinters
    in the fireplace and blows on them.
When a tongue of fire blazes up, she places
    some small pieces of coal
    on the little wooden tent.

"Oh, that looks good," Mama says.

"Feels good, too," I say.

Baby Mary starts whining to get out of bed.

Mama wraps her in a quilt and carries her to the
chair by the fire.

I add more coal, then set a pot of water to heat.

When all the coal is on the fire, I put on my coat
again.

Baby Mary wiggles her hands toward the fire
and says, "Goo, goo."

"That's too hard on a little boy," Mama says.

"Not as hard as freezing," I tell her.

I stretch tall and say, "See how big I am, big enough
to keep us warm through a little old cold spell."

Then I tell her, "You have us some breakfast after
a while, Mama."

Each time I go up the hill it gets a little easier.
Each time I get to the coal bank I speak to the
   roof-rock, since it seems a nice thing to do.
Along about sundown I say, "Thank you, you little
   old coal bank. Now I got to quit for a while."

We sit near the hearth and talk about all kinds of
   things, and sing a song or two.
Mama says, "This'll be the coldest night you ever saw,
   if the wind doesn't blow us all away."
After we go to bed, I listen to the wind howling
   around the roof and squeezing through the cracks.
When it puffs down the chimney, the flames of fire
   climb higher and chase it away.

Mama," I say, "you think this old house will
stand up all night?"

"Oh, I think so," she answers. "Anyway, let's hope
it does."

The house is there looking just the same the next
    morning.
"Maybe I better go up and see about some more coal,"
    I tell Mama.
"You like that," Mama says.
"Maybe I do," I say.

The roof-rock has fallen, and the coal bank is gone.
The big tree has smashed down over it.
Some of the branches have broken into
    a lot of pieces.
"Thank you for waiting to fall at night,"
    I say to the rock and the tree.

The wind has gone away.
The sun is in the sky, making the world
bright and warm.
I load the wagon with small pieces of wood.
"A good bunch of firewood," I say,
"and we be warm now.
We be toasty warm
till springtime comes."

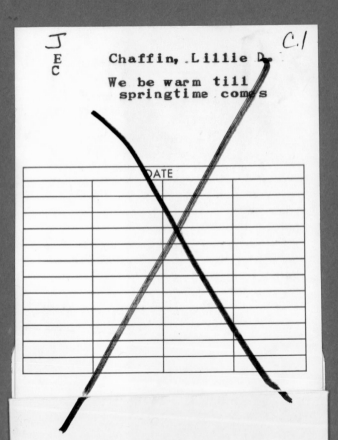